THE CREATURE IN THE DARK

Something was making them angry. Something was making them scared. First they barked, trying to be brave. Then they growled, deep in their throats. Then they whined, and slunk away, tails down.

'What the—?' shouted Dad, starting forward at a run. Sammy ran with him. The woolly bundle was half a sheep. It had been dead quite a long time . . .

The dead sheep is only the beginning. Other animals die or go missing and a great black creature is seen vanishing into the night. But who or what is the killer? And how can anyone stop it?

Thriller Firsts is an exciting series of fast-paced adventure stories especially for younger readers of the seven to nine age group. With clear, straightforward text and plenty of illustrations they are ideal for every child who loves a good, gripping read.

Robert Westall was born in Tynemouth, Northumberland. He studied Fine Art at Durham University and University College, London, and then became head of Art and Careers at Sir John Deane's College, Cheshire where he worked until he left to become an antique dealer in 1985. He is very highly regarded as a children's author—*The Machine Gunners* won the Carnegie Medal and the Horn Book Boston Globe Honor Award, *Scarecrows* also won the Carnegie Medal and *Devil on the Road* was a runner up for the same award. Robert Westall's other books for children include *The Wind Eye, Fathom Five, Break of Dark, The Haunting of Chas McGill, The Cats of Seroster, Futuretrack Five* and *Urn Burial*.

Other titles in the series

THRILLER FIRSTS

THE CREATURE IN THE DARK

Robert Westall

Illustrated by Liz Roberts

Blackie

British Library Cataloguing in Publication Data

Westall, Robert
The creature in the dark.—(Thriller
firsts).
I. Title   II. Roberts, Elizabeth
III. Series
823'.914 [J]   PZ7

ISBN 0-216-92427-8

Blackie and Son Ltd
7 Leicester Place
London WC2H 7BP

Typesetting by Jamesway Graphics, Middleton, Manchester
Printed in Great Britain by Thomson Litho Ltd, East Kilbride, Scotland

Chapter One

They were all waiting for Dad to come, so they could start twelve o' clock dinner. They heard his boots clinking across the farmyard cobbles, quick and angry. Somebody was in for it!

Sammy shuddered a bit, and wriggled his bottom on the long settle. What had he done since yesterday that Dad might have found out?

Dad came through the open sunlit door like a thunderbolt. His face was white with rage, making the whiskers on his chin stand out like a dark cloud. His big fists were clenched, like he was going to start a fight.

But his fierce blue eyes just skimmed across Margie's face, then Sammy's, then Mam's. Nobody in this house was in trouble, this time. Sammy felt Margie relax, on the settle next to him. Mum gave a tiny sigh of thanks, just a quiet breath really.

'I'll have me dinner, Missus!'

Mam was quick, getting it out of the oven.

Until Dad's rage was out, anybody could still cop it. Mam said, very gently, 'What's up, love?' Like she was handling one of them time-bombs the Jerries were dropping on London, that they read about in the paper.

'Damn that Joe Hoskins. His fence is broke again. Ten of his cows trampling my corn in top field.'

Mam made gentle worried noises; not words. Not words that Dad could pick a fight with.

6

'I'll have Hoskins this time. I'm reporting him to the War Ag!'

Sammy sucked in his breath. The War Ag was a terrible thing. The War Ag lived in Penrith, and in London as well. It belonged to Mr Churchill and the King. It could do anything. It could throw farmers off their land, even when they *owned* it. The War Ag was so terrible, even Mam tried to argue.

'Joe—if you tell on him—they'll throw him out for sure. With all those little bairns. Where will they go?'

'That's his worry. He should have thought of that before. His farm's a wreck—just growing thistles, blowing their seed onto *my* fields.'

'Who'll run it, then?'

Dad stopped looking angry. The red patches came back into his cheeks. He gave a sly grin. 'Maybe they'll give it to me, Missus! I'm nearest. I could use that land.'

Sammy sat and stared at him, all mixed up. It would be good to have more land. All good farmers wanted more land. But where would Billy and Sheila Hoskins go when their Dad was thrown off his farm? To the cities like London and Manchester, where the German bombers came every night? Where everything was smashed-up and burning? Where there weren't enough houses left even for the townies to live in?

But what worried him more was his Dad. You were supposed to love your Mam and Dad; the Bible said so.

He loved Mam all right.

But when Dad was angry, Sammy was just plain scared of him. And when he had that sly greedy look on his face, Sammy just wished someone else was his Dad. Someone like Uncle Artie.

*　　　*　　　*　　　*　　　*

The men from the War Ag came a week later. In their own big, black car. Two tall, grim men, in long, grey overcoats and black hats. They stopped at Sammy's farm, to ask the way to Hoskins' in posh townie voices. Sammy, swinging on the gate, couldn't understand what they said, till they'd said it three times.

Their sharp eyes were everywhere, from the

farmyard cobbles to the house's chimneys. Sammy was glad *their* farmyard was tidy, the cow-muck piled neatly in the midden, the hens big and fat. But there was a bit of rope lying by the gate. Sammy wanted to run over and pick it up, and say sorry. But he didn't dare move.

One man said to the other, 'This farmer's good—do you think he could run Hoskins'?'

'We'll offer it to him,' the other replied. 'He'll not refuse, if we pay him well. I never knew a farmer refuse land or money.'

They both laughed, sneeringly, as if Sammy wasn't even there. Then they got back in their big car and drove on to Hoskins'.

Another week later, the Hoskins left. They drove off in their old lorry that was piled high with pink mattresses, chairs and pots and pans tied together with string.

Sammy was swinging on the gate again, as they passed. Only, the lorry broke down opposite the gate. Hoskins' lorry was always breaking down, because he tried running it on paraffin instead of petrol, since petrol was hard to get. It stank like burning rags, even when it was going.

Mr Hoskins got down to fiddle with the engine. Mrs Hoskins just sat in the cab, blinking and blowing her nose every two minutes, on a very wet hanky. The kids, Billy and Sheila, sat among the furniture on the back, as if they were sitting inside their castle. It looked quite good fun, being up there with the wind blowing your hair and the country-side streaking past.

But they weren't enjoying it. They were just staring at nothing, seeing nothing, sitting quite still. They looked like the French refugees in the war films.

Sammy waved shyly. They didn't wave back. Sheila tried to smile, but her face went all peculiar, and she turned away out of sight.

Mr Hoskins *couldn't* get the engine to start. He was no good with engines. He was no good with most things.

Then Dad came charging out of the house. He pretended to be all friendly with Mr Hoskins, slapping him on the back and saying he would help him mend the engine in a jiffy.

He did too. Then Mr Hoskins got back into the cab, and shook Dad's hand and said he was a good mate, the best in the world. But if he ever found out who'd told on him to the War Ag, he'd come and kill them with his shotgun . . .

Dad went on smiling. The Hoskins drove away. Sammy often wondered what happened to them, whether the bombers got them, or whether they burned in the Blitz, or whether they starved to death on the tiny food-rations that townies had to live on.

That same morning, Dad walked up to take over Hoskins' farm. He took Sammy with him, as well as the sheepdogs, Brett and Nell. He said Sammy was a big lad now he was eleven. Nearly a man! One day, God willing, both these farms would be his. He was old enough to start learning farming properly!

Sammy thought sadly that Dad just wanted someone to swank to. Dad kept on pointing out with his big knobbly stick all the things that Mr Hoskins had done wrong. The corners of wheatfields were not ploughed properly, so thistles grew five feet tall. There were gaps in the hedges, filled with old bedsteads. The gates sagged so much you had to lift them to

open them. The thin sheep were filthy and the calves had the spreading disease of ringworm on the backs of their necks. Dad kicked all Mr Hoskins' rusty milk-churns over, so they banged and bumped down the silent farm-yard, and ended up in the liquid green filth of the midden.

The empty farmhouse seemed to be watching them, with its blank windows. A curtain moved in the wind, as if somebody was behind it. When they turned a corner, a cloud of terrified hens flapped in their faces, making Sammy's heart leap into his mouth.

But all Dad said was, 'We'll fatten them up for Christmas. They'll never lay decent eggs. I should wring their necks now!'

Why did Dad hate Mr Hoskins so much? Why did he have to show it here? With the empty house and farmyard watching and listening? Everything you said and did was found out in the end. *God* was watching! Mam said so. The vicar said so every Sunday, shouting and thumping the edge of his pulpit, his red face sweating.

But Dad never went to church. Too busy.

Too many cows to milk and fences to see to. Dad only went to harvest festival, and then only so he could boast that the stuff he sent was the best and biggest, and to sneer at what other people sent.

They walked all the way round Hoskins' farm, right to the very top, where the open moor started. There, a thin dirty flock of Mr Hoskins' sheep ran away from Brett and Nell, leaving behind a woolly bundle in the corner between two walls.

Brett and Nell approached it. Until then, they'd been quite happy, waving their tails and sniffing at everything. But now, about six feet away from the woolly bundle, they stopped, each with one front foot held in the air. The hair on their backs went up in a great plumy ridge, and their tails bushed out.

Something was making them angry. Something was making them scared. First they barked, trying to be brave. Then they growled, deep in their throats. Then they whined, and slunk away, tails down.

'What the—?' shouted Dad, starting forward at a run. Sammy ran with him.

15

The woolly bundle was half a sheep. It had been dead quite a long time. The smell was awful, and big, fat, blue flies rose from it, buzzing angrily.

Sammy was no softy. He'd seen sheep mauled to death by townie killer-dogs before. But then they were just a bit cut and bloodied. They looked like they were asleep. Most of them had died from being *run* to death.

But this . . . the front half was all there, untouched, just the neck broken, so that the head lay at a funny angle. And the back part was just gone.

'What the . . . ?' said Dad again, very quietly now. Then he said, 'Look at that leg-bone— bitten straight through wi' one bite. That's no dog.'

'What is it, then?' asked Sammy. He wasn't really frightened yet. He was enjoying asking a question that Dad couldn't answer. Enjoying seeing Dad being upset for a change.

'Oooooh' said Dad crossly. 'It's some rubbish of Hoskins. There's no tellin' what that fool would do. Perhaps he did it himself . . . wanted only half a sheep for his supper.' It was meant to be a joke but it wasn't funny.

Sammy couldn't help staring at the big bone bitten straight through with one bite. What kind of animal, what kind of jaws could do that?

'C'mon,' said Dad, trying to sound all bossy and cheerful again. 'We'll leave it to the crows—they can sort it out.' And he set off back towards Hoskins' farmyard, swinging his stick at thistles and whistling. Brett and Nell were very quick to follow at his heels.

Sammy couldn't tear himself away from staring at the sheep. Then he suddenly realized that Dad was getting a long way away. He panicked and ran till he caught him up.

As they passed Hoskins' house, Sammy noticed the front door was swinging open. 'Leave it', said Dad. 'Nobody's going to live there any more . . .'

Chapter Two

Mam saved Hoskins' hens from having their necks wrung.

Dad went next day to the War Ag at Penrith, to sign papers about Hoskins' farm.

The moment he drove out of the yard, Mam winked at Uncle Artie across the kitchen. Uncle Artie was Mam's younger brother, but he was paid to work on the farm. He was thin and strong and brown, and looked a bit like a cowboy on the movies, with his big beaky nose, and eyes that were wrinkled from squinting against the sun. He wore a big, felt hat all the time, which made him look even more like a cowboy. In the movies Sammy made up in his head, Uncle Artie was always the quick-draw cowboy who gunned down the outlaws, and Sammy was his faithful buddy . . .

Sammy helped Uncle Artie get the hay-trailer fastened to the big Fordson tractor, and they lifted an empty crate on the back. Then all three of them went up to Hoskins'. Uncle

Artie let Sammy drive the tractor. That was
against the law, but Sammy had been driving
the tractor since he was nine. Dad said driving
a tractor wasn't a job for a grown man. Any
kid could do it. Grown men had better things
to do. Dad had had to fit blocks to the tractor's
clutch and brake, so that Sammy's feet could
reach them. But Sammy was a big lad now,
five feet three.

Getting the hens was easy. Uncle Artie
scattered some corn for them, and while they
were eating, he picked them up gently one by

one and passed them to Mam, who popped them in the crate. Uncle Artie was good with all animals. Not like Dad. Every time Dad handled an animal, it turned into a fight. But hens were easy, if you held them right so they couldn't move their wings or legs.

By the time Dad got home, Hoskins' hens were all mixed up with their own in the bottom field. They were all Rhode Island Reds, so Dad couldn't tell which were which. Besides, even Dad had to admit that hens were the farmer's wife's job. She fed them, she sold eggs, she got the money in her purse. Besides, Dad was in a good mood—he'd got the right kind of money out of the War Ag.

Hoskins' pigs and cows weren't so lucky. They went straight to market. Dad reckoned there was something wrong with all of them. The pigs probably had swine-fever and the cows would have something that made them lose their calves. Better to start clean.

The one thing Hoskins had that Dad liked was his big meadow. It lay in a little valley, and the grass was long and rich. Hoskins had never used it. Maybe he'd been saving it for hay. Dad said it was just the place for the Cheviots.

Dad kept two kinds of sheep—Cheviots and blackfaces. The blackfaces lived on the high moor. Little, tough, stringy beasts that were terrified of you. You couldn't get within twenty yards of them, without a dog to help. You only saw them once a year, when you brought them down off the moor to shear their wool, and dip them and count them. The rest of the year, they lived and died alone. In a bad winter, dozens died in blizzards.You didn't know till you found their skeletons the next spring. But they cost nothing to keep, so every one that lived was pure profit.

The Cheviots were different. They were lovely big sheep with white faces and long white ears. They lived in the fields near the farm. They had their lambs in the shelter of the barn, with Uncle Artie staying up all night to look after them. When the snow came, Dad brought bales of hay for them to eat. They were Dad's pride and joy. He went every day to count them and talk to them. After the war, they were going to win prizes in shows.

Sammy went with Dad when he drove them up to Hoskins' meadow. It was a lovely sunny morning. Sammy never forgot the Cheviots going through the gate into the meadow. The grass was so green and the sheep were so white. There were forty-four ewes, and fifty-two well-grown lambs, because some were twins. The lambs were at the playing stage, chasing each other, jumping over each other, and galloping in a crowd. Sammy could never work out why lambs were so full of fun, and why they turned into sheep that were so boring, that just ate and did nothing else at all.

Dad went off to make sure there were no gaps in the stone walls that the sheep could stray out of. Sammy stood looking at Hoskins' house.

And the house looked at Sammy. It sort of . . . hypnotized him. For some reason he was afraid of it. And yet for some reason he had to go in.

It was a mess in the kitchen. Somebody had dropped a pile of cups and saucers by the sink while they were leaving, and just left them in little pieces all over the floor. There were

candles in dribbly beer bottles, an open family Bible, one of Billy's school exercise-books with most of the pages torn out, and a doll of Sheila's with its china face trodden on. The house smelled of Billy and Sheila, who had been good friends, but always a bit pongy. But the smell of them was old and cold, now.

Sammy wandered upstairs. He didn't want to, but he went. He had to see. But there was nothing upstairs except empty brass bed-steads, without their pink mattresses. And one of Sheila's coats still hanging on a nail on her door, and a cap of Billy's. But their smell was stronger. So strong that he muttered, 'Sorry, Billy. Sorry, Sheila,' out loud.

There was another smell, too, mingled with the smell of Billy and Sheila, that he couldn't place . . .

And then he heard a scrabbling on the ceiling overhead.

Sammy ran down those stairs like a streak of lightning. He stood panting in the sunlight of the farmyard, telling himself it must be rats. You always got rats in an empty house. He made himself go back and close the outside

door. He felt it was the least he could do for
Billy and Sheila.

Then Dad called him, and he went home.

*　　　　*　　　　*　　　　*　　　　*

And then the horrible things began to happen.
Dad was too busy now to go every day and
count the Cheviots, so he sent Sammy instead.

The second morning, one of the lambs was
missing. He counted and counted and
counted, but he could only make it fifty-one.

But sheep are hard to count, because they won't stand still. So in the end, he told himself he was just making a mistake, and left it. Dad would go mad if he told him. And if it turned out he had miscounted after all, Dad would give him a good hiding with his belt.

Sammy went up the next day *praying* there'd be fifty-two lambs again.

But this time there were only fifty. He couldn't believe it. He stood there in the sun, sweating and counting, counting and sweating, over and over again. He searched the whole of Hoskins' farm. For gaps in walls, for small woolly bodies, dead or alive. It was *impossible*. Sheep might jump good six-foot stone walls, but lambs never. And the lambs were far too big and strong now for a fox to take. And killer-dogs always left the body.

But still he didn't tell Dad. Dad would ask why he hadn't been told before.

The third morning, Dad went to Penrith market, and left the dogs behind. Sammy took Brett and Nell up with him. To help the search. And because he was scared of something. He didn't know what, but *something*.

26

Another lamb was gone. He could even tell which ewe the lamb had belonged to. Because that ewe was calling for its lamb frantically, and searching backwards and forwards across the field.

But it was Brett and Nell who acted really oddly. They kept running with their noses to the ground, as if following trails of some strange smell. Then they would stop and bark to each other, as if barking warnings. And as their black and white bodies criss-crossed the field, Sammy felt he could almost *see* the invisible creature who had taken the lambs. Brett and Nell were worried, too. Again the long plumes of hair were raised on their backs.

Dad got back from Penrith by three o'clock, pleased as punch with himself. He'd got six good new cows, and ten calves for fattening. He also smelt like a brewery. He was smirking all over his face as he sat on the settle and let Mam pull his boots off for him. He always drank a lot of beer after he'd done well. But Sammy knew that some kids' Dads drank a lot of beer all the time. At least Dad wasn't like *that*.

Sammy knew with a sad heart that there was no way of telling Dad about the missing lambs that wouldn't earn a clout. So he stood close to Dad and said it, braced for the blow.

It came. He wisely went on lying on the floor, so he couldn't be hit again. While Dad raved on about kids who couldn't count straight, and what were schools for, and when *he* was young . . . Then he stormed out.

When Dad came back, he'd stopped raving about kids who couldn't count. He was raving about townie killer-dogs instead. He started getting shotguns out of the cupboard and counting shotgun-shells and shouting for Uncle Artie. He told Sammy he could stay up all night and help, because he was nearly a man now and must learn to bear a man's burdens. Mam tried to argue about Sammy going, but got shouted down. Mam said she would come as well; she was a farmer's daughter, and could shoot as well as any feller. Margie began to cry about being left alone in the house with a killer-dog on the loose.

Dad clouted her. Mam arranged for her to go to Mrs Strong's to sleep. But she went on crying and crying, until even Mam got thoroughly fed up with her.

*   *   *   *   *

Sammy turned up the collar of his thickest jacket. He'd never known a night so cold, even when he helped Uncle Artie with the all-night lambing when the snow was on the ground. Even the inside of his bones felt frozen. His fingers kept going numb, so he was frightened he wouldn't be able to shoot the gun when the time came. He blew on his hands frantically to warm them. He even shoved his fingers in his mouth and tried to suck them warm.

The gun lay on the ground at his feet, fully loaded. Uncle Artie had explained to him where he must *not* shoot—towards the sheep, and at the other corners of the meadow, where Dad and Uncle Artie and Mam were. Shotgun pellets carried a long way; and they could *kill*. Sammy wasn't afraid to shoot the gun. He'd shot many a bunny for the stew pot in his time. But he was scared of what might come over the high stone wall of the meadow, because it wouldn't be a fox and it wouldn't be a townie dog. He remembered that first half-sheep, with its leg-bone bitten straight through.

He was glad Beth was with him. Beth was no more than a half-grown pup, and she was tied up securely, so she wouldn't be shot in the dark by mistake. Just as Dad had Brett and Uncle Artie had Nell tied up. The dogs couldn't move, but if something was coming for the sheep, the dogs would know long before any human . . .

It was a beautiful night, the moon was small and high, and the clouds were like silver lace. The moon picked out every blade of grass in the meadow with silver, and glowed in the thick fleeces of the sheep. He thought he could just see Uncle Artie at the far end of the wall, Mam and Dad were too far away. The sheep lay silent and quiet, and there was just a gentle sound of chewing.

And then, beyond the bulk of the high moors, the fells, the air-raid started. The whole line of the fell-tops was outlined black against silent flashes of light. And then, when the flashes stopped, the dull rumbles started, far away. So far away, you might have thought it was only a thunderstorm.

More flashes, more rumbles. Some poor townies were getting hit—on Tyneside, or West Hartlepool. It was too far north for Leeds or Bradford. Now the flashes were joined by a pink glow in the sky, that kept the fell-tops outlined all the time. Big fires must have started.

A lot of local people often drove up to the fell-tops when they heard a raid start. To see the fun, they said. Mam said it was heartless, making fun out of other people's misery. But there was talk of marvellous firework displays, chains of blue lights in the sky, dropped by the German bombers to light up the targets and German planes shot down like fiery comets.

But it was all so far away. This side of the hills, the only German bombers were those that were running away from the RAF, seeking silence and darkness to crawl away home. One had come down in a field at Nearwathby, still full of bombs. It had blown up in a white sheet of light that had stripped the leaves off the trees for half a mile around. Nobody had been killed except a hut full of chickens. Otherwise, the farmers' war was against the inspectors from the War Ag . . . who would send you to jail for selling a townie two dozen eggs.

God, he could hear a plane now! High up, coming over the fell. You could tell it was a German, because the engines went 'doodge, doodge, doodge' whereas the RAF planes made a steady drone.

His eyes scanned the sky frantically. Then he saw it, because there was a light aboard it. Or . . . a little streak of flame from one of the engines. It seemed to be heading straight for him. Suppose it crashed? Suppose it was still full of bombs, like the one at Nearwathby? Or suppose it just dropped its bombs anywhere, to get rid of them, like the one at Knarsby?

His heart in his mouth, Sammy watched the monster grow. It had two engines, a nose that shone like glass in the moonlight, and it was black, with a black cross on its side.

This bomber was really not very well. It flew twisted, with one wing down, like a half-swatted fly. The line of fire from one engine grew longer. Behind, a trail of black smoke made the moonlit clouds dirty. He

33

could hear one engine going steady, and the other one sort of screaming. It couldn't be a quarter of a mile away.

At his feet, Sammy felt Beth growl and crouch against his leg. It must be pretty scary for her too.

Then the bomber seemed to get better. The line of fire went out. The screaming note stopped. The machine turned south, flashing its cockpits in the moonlight, showing him it was a Heinkel 111, just like in the model magazines. And calmly, as if it had all the time in the world, it made off back over the fells and slowly out of sight.

He breathed a sigh, only partly of relief. If it had come down, there might have been souvenirs to show off at school. Or even Jerry fliers to take prisoner with his loaded shotgun. He might have been a hero, in the papers. Ah well . . .

Then he realized that, at his feet, Beth was still tensed, growling. He bent to stroke her. 'It's all right, you silly girl. It's gone, *gone!*'

She went on growling. And she wasn't looking up at the sky. She was trying to peer

through the chinks of the stones in the dry-stone wall.

There was something frightening her on the other side of the wall.

Only then did Sammy remember why he was there. He broke out in a cold sweat all over. His arms and legs began to shake. He tried to pick up the gun with shaking fingers. And it slid, cold and shiny, straight through them. He never knew how he finally got hold of it. But he was frightened to put his fingers on the two triggers, for fear their shaking would make the gun go off.

Beth growled louder, and her nose turned slowly more and more to the right.

Something was walking along the far side of the wall towards him. On soft pads, because it didn't make a sound.

He felt Beth collapse against his leg. Glancing down he saw she was sprawled helpless with sheer terror, her breath coming in great pants.

There came a sound of sniffing through the wall. He and Beth were being sniffed over—by a creature than could break a sheep's thigh-

bone with one bite.

He heard a scrabbling on the other side of the wall.

It was coming over for him!

Something gave him the strength to get the shotgun up, so the barrels rested on top of the wall, where the beast would come. He stared and stared at the top of the wall, and the shiny barrels that were the only thing between him and its terrible teeth, the only thing left in the whole world.

Something black and small appeared above the wall just opposite the shining barrels. With a life of its own, his finger squeezed the triggers.

There was a terrific blinding bang. The gun kicked him in the stomach like he'd never been kicked in football at school. There was nothing left in the world now but the black agony in his stomach. He fell, doubled up against the wall, screaming his head off, with the cold gun useless beneath him.

He came out of a sort of inner whirlwind, to find Uncle Artie shaking him by the shoulder, shouting, 'Are you all right?'

Then Mam and Dad, and Nell and Brett were all there, all shouting and barking and asking dozens of questions. And all he could do was keep on yelling it was on the far side of the wall.

Uncle Artie climbed over, with a torch. He shouted back there was a bit of blood, but not much. And no sign of anything else. Then he said, 'Wait a minute!' And he climbed back over. And in the torchlight, on his hand, there was a smear of blood, and a few black hairs.

'Aye well,' said Dad, with disgust. 'It won't

be back tonight. I suppose you gave it a fright, any road.'

'Our Sammy's only a bairn,' said Mam defensively. 'You expect too much of him . . .'

Dad snorted. 'He had a gun. If only he'd waited . . . now it's all to do again.'

Uncle Artie laid a hand on Sammy's shoulder, kindly. 'First blood to you, Sammy. Maybe it'll go and bother somebody else, after this.'

'It'd *better*,' said Dad bitterly.

And they all trailed home.

Chapter Three

Sammy's Mam kept him off school next day. He felt ill in a way he hadn't felt ill before. No special pain anywhere, but sickish, and aching all over, and very tired. And his eyelid kept twitching, as if a fly kept settling on it. He lay on the settle in front of the kitchen range, and although the sun was shining outside, he was glad of the fire. He didn't want to go outside. He didn't like it when Mam went out to feed the chickens. He was glad when she came back and started doing the ironing. There was a big pile of ironing. It would keep her in the kitchen with him till well past dinner-time.

He tried not to think about the night before. But his mind kept touching it, then running away. The way Beth had shaken and fallen down with fear. The sniffing though the chinks in the stone wall. And he kept listening for that sniffing to start again, round the house. Even in daylight. And he worried about Uncle Artie. Where was he? What was he doing?

Had he his gun with him? He had awful visions of Uncle Artie mending a fence somewhere, leaving his gun lying against a post, and working further and further away from it, and the black thing creeping up on him. He even worried about Dad a bit, though Dad had driven in to Penrith in the Vauxhall. Could the black thing get inside a car?

He was glad when he heard Uncle Artie's voice outside. He was talking, or rather shouting, to a deep rumbly voice: Sergeant Hargreaves the policeman. And then Sergeant Hargreaves came into the kitchen with Uncle Artie, looking strange with his red hair flattened and his helmet under his arm. Mam looked up from her ironing.

'You oughta hear this!' said Uncle Artie, all excited.

Sergeant Hargreaves was little and old for a policeman, quiet and not bossy. All the farmers liked him. He didn't make trouble, like most policemen. If he caught a farmer at harvest time running his tractor and trailer without lights in the dusk, he didn't put him in court for it. Just gave him a good telling-off,

warning him not to let it happen again. He was a farmer's son from Langwathby. He knew how hard life could be for farmers.

'Cup of tea, sergeant?' said Mam. She always had the black kettle simmering on the hob.

'Don't mind if I do,' said the sergeant, settling in Dad's big kitchen chair and making himself comfortable.

'Tell her,' said Uncle Artie, still fiddling about, he was so excited.

'This black beast that's been takin' your lambs,' said the sergeant, 'they saw it last night. Tommy Stevenson an' his Missus. They'd been up on't fell, watching air-raid. In't car. It crossed the road in front of 'em when they were coming back . . .'

'What was it?' asked Mam. She reached for the kettle, with a hand that trembled.

'Couldn't tell. You know how dim head-lights have to be for the blackout. But they said it was black. Bigger'n an Alsatian . . .'

'Tell her what it had in its mouth!' said Artie, swallowing.

'All in good time,' said the sergeant, placidly. 'Well, missus, they said it had a young calf. Dead. Looked like its neck was broken. And it jumped clean over the hedge, still carrying it.'

'Gerraway,' said Mam. 'What kind of thing could carry a calf?' But her voice was shaky.

'I've checked,' said the sergeant. 'One of Mason's two-week-old calves is missin'.'

Mam turned pale. 'If it could take a calf, it could take a bairn.'

'That's what we're scared of. Tommy Stevenson got out o't' car and went to have a look for it, the damn fool. But he didn't see owt more.'

'What sort of animal?' Sammy could tell Mam was worrying about Margie, coming home from school for dinner.

'I've checked over the ground,' said the sergeant. 'It went across the muddy patch by Lewin's duck-pond. Great big prints. Like a cat's, but nigh three inches across. Some big cat out of a circus or zoo. I thought they'd shot them all, when the war started, in case they got loose in the bombings. But they seem to have missed this one. We're getting up a big search tomorrow.'

'He's sent for the Army,' announced Artie. 'They're sending up the Yanks from Lancashire.'

'Give the lazy beggars somethin' to do,' said Mam. 'Make a change from them chasing our girls.'

*　　　*　　　*　　　*　　　*

Heavy engines woke Sammy from a cat-haunted nightmare. He staggered out of bed, his pyjamas falling off his bottom. He pulled back the faded pink curtains, and suddenly felt he was in heaven.

The village green was jam-packed with green jeeps and lorries, with big white stars on them. There was even a sort of half-tank, with wheels at the front and tank-tracks at the back, and a real machine-gun. There were swarms of soldiers wearing funny gaiters on their legs, and steel helmets like eggs.

The Yanks had come. He was dressed and out the front door before he knew it. But other kids were already there, chewing gum they'd scrounged. Sammy wandered through the trucks in awe, chewing gum himself, for the

soldiers had pockets full of it and gave it to you before you asked for it. They were all in a good mood, slapping their guns and calling it a tiger-hunt. Like kids on holiday.

At last he was hauled back by Mam for his breakfast. All the soldiers were very polite to Mam, calling her 'Ma'am' and frequently saluting her. Far more polite than they were to their own officers, whom they called 'Jack' or 'old Buddy'.

'They ain't got no discipline,' said Mam. 'Not real soldiers at all—chewing gum like that. God help us if they have to fight the Germans.'

Sammy played with his breakfast. Then Dad came in, very full of himself, with an American officer. The officer took off his hat and then saluted, not wearing it. He said he was Captain Schindler, and gave Mam a bag of what he called candies. Mam bobbed her head, embarrassed.

'Captain Schindler's men are doing the Long Wood,' said Dad. 'They want Sammy with them—he knows the place.'

'No,' said Mam, pressing her lips together.

'He's too young.'

'Aw, *Mam*,' wailed Sammy. 'Those *tanks* . . .'

'Aw, Ma'am,' said Captain Schindler. 'He'll be as safe as the First National Bank with us.'

'He's *going*,' said Dad. 'It's his duty. For the War Effort.'

For once, Sammy almost loved Dad.

*   *   *   *   *

Captain Schindler didn't have a tank, but he had a jeep, and a man with a radio gabbling about two company and six company. And a great big truck labelled 'Dodge' full of men who whistled, especially when they passed Sadie Meadows, the land-girl. Sadie seemed pleased. She waved back so hard she nearly rode her bike into a ditch.

They reached Long Wood, and all the Yanks jumped down, stamping their feet and making bets who'd get the tiger. They spread out in a ragged line.

It was then Sammy realized there was no danger of them catching anything. When he came to this wood alone, walking silently in his gym-shoes, the wood was full of life. Rabbits stood up on their hind-legs to sniff the air, even fox-cubs rolled over and over like kittens. Small birds tweeted, wood-pigeons exploded away, knocking down twigs with their strong wings.

But this morning, the wood was an empty silence. Not a thing moved, except great crashing feet and jokes and swearing, and the man with the radio wanting to know where the heck two company was.

Then, halfway through the woods, something zipped past them like an angry bee. A tree straight in front of them exploded in fragments leaving a great scar of sweet-smelling wood.

A heavy hand flung Sammy face-down into the soft moss, almost making him choke.

'Goddam!' said Captain Schindler. 'We're under fire from hostiles!'

'Reckon we found two company, Captain,' said a rude but muffled voice.

*　　　*　　　*　　　*　　　*

Captain Schindler sent Sammy home quick, lying flat in the back of the jeep, where he could see nothing but the ground whizzing past. Mam made him sit on the kitchen floor for the rest of the day, well away from the windows. He sat, listening to bangs in the distance, and neighbours coming in with rumours.

Mrs Malton reckoned it was a pitched battle with German paratroopers, at Renwick road-end.

Mrs Ground had had a burst of machine-gun fire through her washing hanging out to dry.

Mason's best sheepdog came home minus half its tail.

Somebody shot George Trewhitt's bull dead, in his bottom field.

At last the bangs ceased. They watched the Yanks get back into their trucks, looking fed up, and drive away.

Then Dad came home, even more fed up. The Yanks had paid up on the spot for the damage they'd done, with many, many apologies. George Trewhitt had got 500 dollars for his bull, twice what the brute was worth. And he'd sold the corpse to the butcher as prime beef, too. Mason got fifty dollars for his sheepdog's tail, though it would be herding sheep as usual tomorrow. Even Mrs Ground got fifty dollars for her husband's shirts, though he'd go on wearing them, patched.

Dad had had nothing shot at all. Everybody was waving dollars, except him.

Nobody had seen any sign of the black tiger.

*   *   *   *   *

Two weeks passed, and no more lambs or calves went missing. No more cat footmarks were found in muddy places.

'They must've scared it off,' said Dad, one night.

'I'm not surprised,' said Mam. 'They scared everything else . . . they must've scared off God Almighty hisself.'

'It wasn't their fault,' said Dad. 'They did their best. It's them rifles. The bullets carry two miles. A shotgun only carries a hundred yards.'

Everything got back to normal. Farmers stopped carrying their shotguns wherever they went. Kids were allowed to walk to school alone again.

And Sammy went up one night to the meadow, to count the Cheviots. But he took Brett and Nell and Beth with him. He was still nervous. He counted the sheep and lambs. They were all there.

It was on the way home it happened. Walking down the narrow green road, he met the creature coming up towards him. His first, dreamy thought was that it was not as big as a tiger he'd once seen in the zoo.

But it was bigger than the dogs. Longer and higher than an Alsatian, but not so thick in the body. Slim, long-legged, black from nose to tail—shiny black, just like Mason's tom-cat, but the fur was shorter.

It stopped about ten yards away, and looked at him steadily. Its eyes were a very pale green, as cold as ice. For what seemed a long, long time nothing happened. Everything was frozen. Then the black creature looked left, looked right, and then ran straight at Sammy and the dogs.

Beth just fell down, her limbs sprawling in all directions. She was, after all, only a half-grown pup.

But Brett and Nell were wonderful. Their backs went up, their tails plumed, and they went in at the creature, snarling their heads off.

It hissed like a snake, and struck out at them with a paw full of claws, like black lightning.

But they dodged, and came back at it again, one from each side, barking and snarling. And suddenly Beth got up and joined in, barking her little head off. The creature could've killed any one of them, with one blow. But there were three of them, all coming in from

different sides. It couldn't cope with three at once. It backed against a corner of the stone wall. Sammy saw his chance and ran through the gap for home, like he'd never run before, eyes blind so he nearly fell, lungs sucking in air till they almost burst.

Behind him, he could still hear the dogs barking, defending him while he ran away like a coward. He wept for them, because he loved them and the creature would kill them all. Brave Nell, brave Brett, Beth who had been so scared.

When Sammy got home, they couldn't tell what he was saying for five minutes. He couldn't get the words out. He just kept pointing up the green road.

Dad and Uncle Artie and Billy Mason next door ran up the green road like he'd never seen grown men run. He couldn't keep up with them, even though they were carrying their guns . . . Brett! Nell! Beth! . . . He couldn't see for crying.

When they arrived, the dogs were still there. Brett and Nell were still on their feet, though they were panting and sort of dazed, with half-closed eyes. Dad knelt and felt their bodies. Brett had a big patch of blood on his white bib, Nell had lost half her right ear, and the blood had run down the side of her face. They were all covered in little spots of blood, from scratches. But Dad, oddly gentle for once with his hands, reckoned they'd live. They were not hurt badly.

Beth was still breathing, but her eyes were shut and wouldn't open. Dad carried her down the hill, getting his grey shirt all covered in blood. He drove her straight to the vet's at Penrith.

Again, the black creature was gone.

*   *   *   *   *

Beth did not die. After a fortnight, Dad brought her home from the vet's, saying in a grumbly voice that she'd cost a fortune, and would never work sheep again. She limped around the kitchen, licking everybody's hand, glad to be home. Mam made her a bed by the stove, a big cardboard box with an old blanket inside, and she soon got into it, gratefully.

Dad grumbled again that she'd cost a

fortune. Mam gave him a straight look.

'She saved your bairn,' she said. 'She'll never lack a place in this kitchen while I'm livin' an' she'll get rabbit-meat every day.'

Meanwhile, there was another hunt for the creature. Much better this time. Police, farmers with shotguns, shepherds who knew the moors like the backs of their hands and trained marksmen from the Durham Light Infantry, from over Barnard Castle way. Nobody fired a shot. Dad's hopes of getting money out of the Army were dashed.

Good and thorough and quiet though they'd been, there was no sign of the creature. But again, they must have frightened it away. No more farm animals died.

Life went back to normal.

Chapter Four

A month passed. Then, in spite of Mam making a fuss, Dad sent Sammy up to count the Cheviots again.

They were all there. But it was such a lovely evening that he dawdled on the way home. He sat on a bank to watch the rabbits playing and feeding in the nearly flat rays of the sunset. They were all gold down one side.

It was so peaceful.

Then suddenly he felt he was being looked at. He glanced to his right, and the creature was standing only yards away, looking at him with those eyes like green ice.

Sammy knew he hadn't a chance. If he tried to run, it would have him in a flash. He knew it could run much faster than he could. So he just went on sitting there and looking at it.

His body felt oddly peaceful, unable to move. His eyes seemed extra sharp, so he could see every hair of the creature, the way the hairs made patterns round its nose and eyes. The way the sun shone pinkly through the thin hair of the ears, which were rounded, not pointed like the cat's at home.

The creature padded up to him. Oddly, its claws weren't out.

It came so close he could see the long black whiskers on each side of its blunt nose. Its breath on his face, as it sniffed him, was cool and sweet. He could see nothing now but the great green eyes. He imagined the huge teeth, under those velvet lips.

Its cold, cold nose touched his nose. It made

a noise deep in its throat, not a growl or a snarl, more like a rough purr.

And then with one swift movement, it had rolled over and lay sprawled against him, tummy uppermost, staring at him with upside-down eyes. Almost like the cat at home, wanting its tummy tickled.

It reached out one long paw, and tapped his face, gently, questioningly.

Hardly daring to breathe, Sammy reached out a hand and stroked the creature's belly, ever so gently. The rough purring increased.

He noticed that it was a female, a female feeding its young, because its rows of black nipples were swollen and surrounded by patches of bare skin, and there were soft mounds under the nipples.

And as she wriggled with joy under his stroking, he knew she wasn't a circus or zoo animal.

She was somebody's pet.

*   *   *   *   *

Sammy never knew how long he sat there in the sunset. It was like a strange heaven. He stroked, the creature purred, while his mind made sense of it all in a series of jumps.

The animal's long legs and body gave him a clue. This must be a cheetah, only for some reason she was black. He knew from history lessons that the Egyptians had kept cheetahs as pets, and used them as hunting-dogs. This one would kill lambs and calves, because she was hungry. But she wouldn't attack people. That other night, when he and the dogs had thought they were being attacked, she'd probably been trying to get away in fear, because she was trapped by the high walls of the narrow green road. That terrible fight had all been a mistake.

But in the end, she showed him why she'd really tried to run past him up the green road. She rolled over and got up, made a questioning purr at him, and ran ten yards up the road. Then she stopped and looked back. She wanted him to follow, to show him something.

Sammy went with her. All the way back to Hoskins'. Right up to the farmhouse itself. She didn't try the closed door. She went round the back, leapt onto the low kitchen roof, and vanished in through an open window. He could see by the mass of claw-marks on the edge of the kitchen roof that that was the way she always used.

He let himself in through the front door. The smell in the house was different. It still smelt of Billy and Sheila, and the smells of any empty house—damp and mould, and rat-droppings. But there were also new smells, a warm, furry, animal smell, and the smell of old meat.

There were muddy cat paw-marks on the bare wooden stairs. He followed them up. There was a big trapdoor in the hall ceiling, pushed to one side, showing darkness, and the chinks of light between the slates of the roof. There were more claw-marks on the edge of the trapdoor, where she'd jumped up. And out of the darkness came a stirring, a clawing, a mewing.

He had to search for Hoskins' old step-ladder, before he could get up to the ceiling. Lucky they hadn't taken it with them. He poked his head through the trapdoor. The smell of old meat nearly made him choke. The first thing he saw, in the dim light from the chinks between the slates, was a lot of old bones, skulls of animals and bare rib-cages.

But beyond, on a rough pile of clawed-up old blankets and shredded newspaper, three small, round, black creatures, struggled mewling to their wobbly feet.

The cheetah glanced at him, her eyes glowing like green mirrors in the gloom. Then she threw herself down on her side, and the three small, round bodies crawled in between her legs, and settled in a furry mass, with their noses against her belly, pummelling her with their short, strong legs. A storm of tiny purring and sucking broke out, and above it the deeper rougher purr of the mother.

Sammy watched, in heaven. Again, he didn't know how long he watched. Till he suddenly realized it was getting dark, and Mam was expecting him home for supper.

'Bye bye!' he said to the cheetah. Then he was down the ladder, and running for home in the darkening dusk.

And as he ran, he began to be afraid. No longer afraid *of* the creature. But *for* the

creature. For the whole little family was so far from any home they might ever have known. Surrounded by dogs and farmers with guns, and soldiers.

He approached his own door like a thief, like a traitor or a spy. If he ever let slip what he knew, the cheetah and her cubs would be shot within the hour. His lips must not only be sealed, but locked and barred and bolted, awake and asleep. Forever and ever. . .

He approached his own door a very lonely stranger. This was something he couldn't even tell Uncle Artie.

*   *   *   *   *

Sammy didn't sleep much that night. He sat at the open window and watched the dawn break, a thing he'd never done before in his life. But as the pearly grey light flooded through the village and farmyard, and all the birds began to sing, he felt peaceful at last. He knew there were three things he had to do. Besides keeping his mouth shut.

First, he must get a lock on that farmhouse door, and nail up all the windows on the ground floor. He knew that hardly anyone went near the house now. His father, because of what had happened to Joe Hoskins, avoided the place like the plague. And no other farmer would go there, because Dad got very nasty with trespassers. But there was always the odd wandering tramp. And they said army deserters were roaming the country, living rough.

Second, he must feed the cheetah. With rabbits. He was a country boy. He'd known how to snare rabbits since he was seven. He knew the right places to set the snares, though he hadn't done it much lately. If he gave her enough fresh rabbits, she would leave the lambs and calves alone. She might even get a taste for rabbit, and start hunting them for herself. Maybe she was living on rabbits already. Maybe that was why there'd been no reports of missing farm animals. But he'd take no risks. If lambs began going missing again, there'd be another search. The thought of her being so near the Cheviots brought him out in a cold sweat.

But even if he did all that, she still wouldn't be safe for long. The young cubs would grow.

And it would be hard enough to feed one grown cheetah, let alone four. So the third thing he had to do was to get help from the outside world. He must try and find her owner. But *how*? How far had she come, before she ended up here? From the towns? From the bombing? It must have been the bombing that blew open her cage and released her to wander the countryside. Perhaps she came from Tyneside? Manchester? London? How on earth could he reach *them*?

At last it came to him.

He would write to the newspapers. In his very best handwriting. So they would think he was a grown-up, and take him seriously.

Chapter Five

Sammy was allowed to go into Penrith on Saturday mornings, to change his library books. Dad grumbled. He needed Sammy round the farm to help every hour that wasn't wasted in school. But Mam said if Sammy wasn't allowed to go to the library he wouldn't pass the exam for the High School. And Dad wanted Sammy to go to the High School so he could swank about it in the pub. Hardly anybody in the village had ever gone to the High School.

So, five days later, Sammy went. He sat back in the bus, and thought that things had gone pretty well. He'd caught a lot of rabbits, and the cheetah had eaten them all. She could eat about three at one go, crunching them like sweets and eating them fur and all. Nobody had made a fuss about farm animals being taken, though he had found the fresh carcass of one yearling lamb in the loft, the last time he went. And the smell of old meat from the loft was starting to be bad in Hoskins' farmyard.

He had nailed up all the windows, and the doors from the inside. And he had pinched a letter Dad had kept from the War Ag, with the War Ag's official address on it. He'd crossed out with blue crayon what the War Ag had said, and put on the blank part of the paper, in very neat lettering, 'KEEP OUT—BEWARE FALLING BRICKS'. Pinned to Hoskins' front door, it looked quite proper and official.

Sammy got into the house now by ladder from the kitchen roof, just like the cheetah.

When he got to Penrith, he went straight to the newsagents, and bought a packet of envelopes, and a pad of lined writing paper. Then he went into the library, changed his books, and then went into the reading room, a place he never usually went. He had to have the newspapers they kept there, so he could get their addresses. He had already got the address of the *Daily Mail* which Dad bought. He had found the address with great difficulty, at the bottom of the right-hand column on the back page. He thought all the other papers' addresses would be in the same place. The reading-room was awful. It was full of little old men in caps and mufflers, coughing and smoking, and every paper was in the hands of a little old man. They seemed to be only interested in the racing page and the football page. They were talking about betting and doing the pools.

As soon as one little old man put down a paper, another snatched it up. There were crowds of them, hanging round in the corners waiting, like flocks of old black crows. The clouds of cigarette smoke made Sammy cough, and he was in despair. He only had an hour and a half, as he had to be home for dinner by one o'clock.

He drifted back miserably to ask the lady at the desk to help him.

And then he saw them. *Another* pile of newspapers, looking old and torn-edged, tied up in a bundle with coarse hairy white twine.

'Please Miss, can I see them papers?' He put up his hand, like he did with the teacher at school.

She smiled. 'They're yesterday's, sonny. They're going for salvage, for the War Effort!'

'*Please*, Miss, can I read them? We don't get no newspapers in our house—me Dad can't afford it. And I've got to write an essay for school—on the War Effort.'

He never usually lied, even to Dad. Even though it sometimes meant a thrashing. So he lied pleasingly, blushing. With another smile, the woman gave in, and handed across the bundle. 'Just you be sure you keep them together. And tie them up neatly afterwards.'

He carried them back to the reading-room in triumph and found a tiny corner to sit in.

But the moment he opened the bundle, the old men pounced and started pinching them off him. He kept yelling desperately, 'They're yesterday's, mister. Yesterday's!'

But the old men took no notice. They took the lot. And then they began tossing them back at him, blaming him because they were yesterday's.

At last he got them all back, found the addresses and copied them out. He started on his first letter, in his very best handwriting. It was very hard to know what to say. He would have to put a false address, but it had to be somebody's *real* address. He didn't dare have reporters from the newspapers coming to his own house, or the game would be up. He didn't dare sign his own name, or Dad would thrash the truth out of him, as soon as the first reporter called. He had to give the name of somebody who knew all about the lost lamb business, the black tiger business. Somebody bright, who the reporters would take notice of. Somebody important.

Squire Willowby. At Willowby Manor . . . no, that was no good. Squire Willowby was too famous. He had a telephone. They'd ring him up and he would say he'd never written the letters, and the newspapers wouldn't come. They'd think it was a hoax.

Old Billy Bragg at Renwick. He was bright. He knew all the gossip, and he wasn't on the phone. And he was interested in strange things about the countryside. Once he'd told Sammy about the old Roman lead mines on the fell.

So, tongue sticking out of the corner of his mouth, in his very best handwriting, Sammy began,

'Dear Sir,

Have you heard about the big black cheetah that is killing farm animals around here? It has taken many lambs, and a young calf. It has been seen carrying a dead calf in its mouth. It leapt over a hedge carrying the calf in its mouth.

But the truth is that it is tame. It is somebody's pet. I have stroked it. And it has young—three cubs. Can you help to find the owner, and get it to somewhere safe? It is a beautiful animal, and very friendly to hu-

mans, even if it does kill sheep and calves to stay alive.'

That sounded all right. That sounded like Billy Bragg might have written it. He looked up, relieved, triumphant. Only to see with horror that the kind lady from the desk was bearing down on him, a beaming smile on her face.

'And how are we getting on with our history of the war?' she asked.

Sammy slammed his writing pad shut, as quick as if he was swatting a fly.

The lady frowned. 'Aren't you going to show me?' She looked hurt, and she was a kind lady. Sammy felt ashamed. But he thought of the cheetah, and hardened his heart.

'No,' he said. 'It's a secret. It's about the War Effort.'

The lady did not look so friendly now. Her lips were pressed in a tight line, like the headmistress's when someone had done something bad.

'Well, young man, if it's *so* secret, I think you'd better do it somewhere more secret than *my* library. You've caused a lot of fuss this morning. I've had all my old gentlemen complaining about you. Come on, gather up those papers tidily. And make *sure* you fasten them together properly.'

She stood over Sammy till he was finished, and then showed him to the door and held it open for him.

Oh, well, he thought, I can still write the letters in the park. There's a bench. But when he got outside, it was pouring with rain, and he only had half an hour till his bus.

What about the post office? There were places to write in there. But they were too high up for him, the post office shelves. And people were waiting to use them, peering over his shoulder to see what he was writing and saying, 'Hurry up, kid. You going to be all day?'

It was no good. And it was ten minutes to his bus. In desperation he bought enough stamps for the letters. Then he had to run hard all the way to the bus, and only just caught it.

He tried writing on the bus. But he was panting and shaking all over, and the bus

joggled, and the writing came out untidily. He'd ruined three envelopes before he stopped. Then he just sat, and let the bus carry him, and all the stuff his Dad must never see, right to his own front door.

Mam was standing at the front door, watching for him. She waved and shouted, 'Dinner's ready.'

So he had to walk up right to the front door, holding the stuff hidden inside his biggest library book. It made the book bulge. She was bound to notice. She always looked to see what books he'd got out. Disaster gaped.

And then Sammy saw the door of the outdoor toilet.

'Just a minute, Mam. I'm bustin'.' And he ran for the toilet door, pushed home the latch and was safe.

You see, Dad had had an indoor toilet put in, a year ago. The only indoor toilet in the whole village. Something else to brag about.

But Mam kept the outdoor toilet sweet. And only Sammy still used it. It was built onto the end of the house and almost smothered in ivy. Ivy grew further across the door every week. You had to push it aside to get in. And ivy curled inside too, through the gap between the walls and the roof. Sammy spent hours in there, just dreaming, because it was the one private place in the house. If you were on the toilet, you could think in peace. And if they yelled for you, you could always yell back, 'I'm not finished yet.' And there was nothing they could do about it.

Mam worried that Sammy was constipated, and he was dosed regularly with senna pods.

But it was a small price to pay for your own peace and quiet. The chance to watch the little pools of sunlight that came through the peep-hole in the door. Sometimes little shadows of clouds drifted across the patches of sunlight, like tiny movies.

He got out his pad and his envelopes, and pushed them behind the thick ivy that grew over the top of the cistern. Safe.

He emerged fastening the buckle of his belt.

He nearly forgot to wash his hands before he sat down to dinner.

*   *   *   *   *

After that, it worked like a charm. He smuggled in a bit of smooth plank to rest on his knees, and even a spare bottle of ink, hidden behind the ivy. It took him a week, but he wrote the letters beautifully. Mam just thought he was more constipated than usual, and gave him a double dose of senna pods. But on the evening when he slipped the wad of letters into his pocket, and strolled down to the postbox set in the wall of the village post office, he thought it was well worth it.

Just then, old Tom Crumble came round
the corner without warning, and saw him put
the letters in, but he only said, 'You a-writing
to your sweetheart, Sammy?'

And Sammy said, 'It's Uncle Artie's birthday, Tuesday.' Which thank God it was, and
Sammy bought him a smashing birthday card
the next day, to cover up the story.

And so it was done. Over the next few days,
Sammy often thought about his letters winging
their way around the country, to the *Manchester
Guardian*, *News Chronicle* and *Daily Herald*.

But he had a lot more to think about too. It was the start of the summer holidays. The hardest working time of the year. There was the hay harvest to get in, then the sheep to shear and dip, and last of all the corn harvest. Day after day he drove the tractor. Day after day he lurched around the loose wobbly hay on top of the hay-cart, trying to arrange the bundles that the men forked up, so that the load wouldn't fall off the cart on the way to the barn. The men thought it was a good joke to hit him with their bundles and knock him over. He'd long since learnt to dodge. Hay seeds got in his eyes and the palms of his hands blistered with the smooth cracked wood of the hay fork till they bled.

But tired though he was, so tired he fell asleep in his chair over tea, he kept faith with the cheetah. Early and late he visited his snares, and there were always plenty of young rabbits in them. This time of year you could hardly walk in the fields without falling over a rabbit. Sometimes he was so tired he didn't even see the cheetah. Just threw the rabbits on to the kitchen roof.

But they were always gone the next time he went.

*   *   *   *   *

Then the reporters came; four in one old beaten-up car. Not from the big papers, but from the Penrith and Carlisle papers. But what they wrote would go in the big papers.

Anyway, they sat in a lot of farm kitchens, and drank an awful lot of tea, after they'd asked for something stronger and been offered elderberry wine. They listened carefully, and wrote it all down in their notebooks, which were full of strange squiggles and hook-shapes. They were disappointed the black tiger hadn't been seen for a month. But they showed no interest in stirring out of the farm kitchens to go up into the fields to see for themselves. They said it would be worth a few lines, worth a few bob. Dad and Uncle Artie had their pictures taken, with shotguns under their arms, pointing vaguely up at the moor. Then the reporters went away again.

But their articles did well. The government

censors let them be printed because they were no help to the Germans. (Except one by a fool who said perhaps the Germans were dropping the black tigers by parachute from bombers, to kill off British cows.) Dad made a collection of the articles in an old scrapbook (with the photo of him and Uncle Artie on the front). There were headlines like 'KILLER CAT TERRIFIES VILLAGE', which gave everybody a good laugh.

Then the Battle of Alam Halfa got under way. And everyone forgot about the cheetah. There was no fresh hunt for her.

She'd been scared away hadn't she? Probably dead of cold and wet in some ditch.

Two weeks passed, and nobody came to claim her.

Chapter Six

It all went wrong one Sunday dinner-time.

The corn harvest was in. It was nearly time for harvest festival again. The harvest had been good. Even Dad was in a good mood and had taken Uncle Artie to the pub before lunch.

Everyone was happy but Margie.

'I'm bored,' she whined.

'I'll bore you,' said Dad. 'There's a lot of eggs need washin'.'

'Sammy doesn't play with me any more. He always says he's *busy*.'

Every eye turned on Sammy. It was true. He used to take Margie with him, snaring rabbits and things, and gathering mushrooms. But not since . . . Sammy hardened his heart by thinking about the cheetah, and lied again. He made his face sulky on purpose.

'Girls is *boring*,' he said. 'She always starts whining about how tired she is. And she's scared of gettin' her shoes muddy, or tearin' her frock.'

Margie's mouth dropped open at such terrible lies. She had never been a moaner.

'I never did,' she said, and started to cry.

'I want to go blackberrying,' she said. 'Up Hoskins'.' She sniffed loudly. 'The berries are as big as raspberries and I want some blackberry jelly.'

'I'm glad Hoskins' is good for somethin',' said Dad. 'I could do wi' some nice bramble jelly, Missus. Hey, Sammy, you take your sister blackberryin' up Hoskins' this afternoon. No argie-bargie. That's an *order*.'

And there was no getting out of it.

Sammy got some jam-jars ready, putting string round the necks to make carrying-handles, feeling very fed up. And then they set off.

Thank God the bramble-bushes she had her eye on were at the far end of Hoskins'. But the wind was blowing from the house, and although it was only a gentle late August breeze, Sammy could swear he could smell that smell of old meat.

Well, at least with the breeze blowing that way, the cheetah probably wouldn't smell *him*.

He hadn't fed her today yet. She'd be hungry. She was thin, now, with every rib showing, however many rabbits he gave her. Those cubs were draining the life out of her. And she had an incredible sense of smell. Often she met Sammy when he was carrying rabbits, when he was still a long way from the house. She would just suddenly appear, noiselessly, rub her head against his leg, and then demolish most of the rabbits on the spot, just taking away one in her mouth for the cubs.

Anyway, they started picking blackberries. They were big and juicy like Margie said. Margie cheered up the more she picked. She seemed to have quite forgiven Sammy, though she still grumbled that he didn't talk to her much. Still, she was never short of talk herself. Embarrassing things like whose Mam was having a baby, and whose baby was ill, and what Gertie Bradbury had said to her teacher Miss Jackson, cheeky thing.

Sammy was too busy to talk. He was just praying non-stop inside his mind that the cheetah wouldn't turn up.

They filled two jars, then four, then six,

which was all they'd brought.

'That'll have to do, I suppose,' said Margie, sounding very like Mam. With a sigh of relief, Sammy grabbed the strings of the six jars and headed for home.

There was a piercing scream behind.

He knew before he turned that the worst had happened.

Margie was standing paralysed, fist in her mouth and screaming, eyes as big as saucers.

The cheetah was casually sniffing the hem of her frock.

*   *   *   *   *

Sammy did what he could. He got the cheetah away from Margie. He tickled the cheetah so that it rolled over on its back and waved its great deadly paws in the air like the cat at home. He said over and over again, 'She's *harmless*, Margie. She's a pet. She's got cubs.'

He even tried bribery. He promised to take Margie everywhere with him. He would give her his big electric torch. And all his Biggles books.

She *seemed* to understand. She *seemed* to

accept the bargain. She wanted the torch and the Biggles books right enough. But she was too pale. Her face looked wrong. She kept on shivering, even after the cheetah, not getting any rabbits, finally went away.

The sun told him, as it lowered towards the west, that it was time for Sunday tea. Being late for Sunday tea wouldn't help.

So he couldn't do anything but take her home. He even considered desperately whether he ought to strangle her, to shut her mouth. But after all, she was still his sister . . . so he cuddled her all the way, whispered the best soothing words he could think of in her ear. But all the time he felt doom approaching, like some terrible, cold thundercloud.

Margie lasted better than he thought. They were lucky. Mam was thrilled to bits with the blackberries, and made a great fuss of them. Dad even said they'd done well. Even when Margie, pale as a ghost, nearly fell asleep over tea, Mam said she was just tired and had overdone it.

They got through the evening, listening to 'Sunday Half-Hour Community Hymn-

Singing' on the wireless. They got to bed. Sammy felt worn out too, like he'd died a thousand deaths. He told himself that by the morning, the memory of the cheetah would be fading in Margie's mind. He fell asleep hoping so.

He was wakened in the middle of the night by Margie screaming. Then he could hear Mam's voice in the corridor outside, and then Dad's.

Mam said, 'She's had a nightmare, poor love.'

He could hear Margie sobbing and mur-
muring.

Ten minutes later, Dad came into his room.

'What's all this about a cheetah, then?' He
was still in his pyjamas, but he had his thick
leather work-belt in his hand.

Chapter Seven

Sammy awakened lying on his tummy. Awakened to the pain. The pain held his backside in an iron cage, so that he dare not move it. While he did not move, the pain was only a dull throb. When he moved, it was like spears thrust into him. His back hurt too, though not so bad. And the backs of his thighs.

He remembered Dad coming in the night, with the belt in his hand and that look on his face, as holy-looking as the vicar preaching, and as gloating as the school bully.

It had been easy to say no to Dad at first. He knew Dad would thrash him whether or not he told him where the cheetah was. So there was nothing to lose. And he was used to being thrashed. But this just went on and on. Every so often, Dad would stop with a look of triumph on his face and say,

'Have you had enough?'

And every time that Sammy shook his head, the triumphant smile would fade, and Dad's eyes go very small, and the beating would start again. And every time Dad's face would go a bit more odd. He would sweat, and the red patches in his cheeks would go small and bright, and his face would sort of . . . wriggle all over. And that big vein would stand out on his forehead.

It had gone on from pain to bigger pain to unbearable pain.

But Sammy had found a secret, a very precious secret.

He found he could separate his mind from his body. While his body screamed, his mind was away in the loft at Hoskins', watching the cheetah feeding her young. His mind was quite safe, up there in the dark loft, Dad could not touch it. And while his mind was safe up there, the cheetah and the cubs were safe up there too.

It stopped when Mam burst in. She mustn't have known what was going on. She must've been busy downstairs getting Margie quiet. Now she stood there, and her face had never looked so grim and white, like a white rock.

'That'll do, Frank,' she said, quietly.

Dad stopped, panting like a dog. He couldn't speak for a bit. Then he said,

'Mind your own business, woman! See to your daughter!'

'I've seen to my daughter. I've come to see to my son!' She came across the bedroom swiftly, and looked at Sammy's backside, and Sammy heard her sudden gasp, nearly a sob. Then she said to Dad,

'You've gone too far this time. If the NSPCC saw that, they'd put you away for life. You're *mad*. You're out of your mind, Frank. You need seein' to.'

Sammy could tell, even through his pain, that Dad was shaken. Dad's voice went all queer and wobbly. Then he said,

'He's my son. Nobody interferes between me and my son!'

'He's *my* son,' said Mam. 'Give him to me, before I send for the police.'

'I give the orders round here!'

'If you touch him again, our Sammy won't *be* here. And neither will Margie, and neither will I. I'll not live wi' you, Frank.'

'Where could you go?'

'Me father's. An' you won't keep this farm long, once me father hears. This farm is me father's. You're only a tenant. And don't you forget it!' Dad let go of Sammy, and blundered out of the door, and thumped off downstairs stamping on every stair as hard as he could.

And Mam had fetched a bottle of yellow stuff, and gently dabbed it on Sammy's backside. It made it hurt more at first, so he could have screamed, but then it settled to a dull throbbing. Mam had murmured to him that he shouldn't defy his Dad. He should obey and respect his father.

And in the end, he slept. Once he'd learnt he mustn't move and must lie on his tummy.

Mam peeped in at him the next morning, and said softly, 'Oh, you're awake then?' and pulled back his curtains on a bright sunny day. She turned to him. 'Sergeant Hargreaves is here, wanting to talk to you. D'you feel up to it? Then I'll get you breakfast in bed . . .'

He nodded. He might as well get it over with.

Sergeant Hargreaves pulled up a little white chair to the bed, and looked sympathetic.

'Not feeling like sitting down, eh?' He
winked. 'Yer Mam told me.' A glow of love for
Sergeant Hargreaves swept over Sammy. He
had a nice wrinkly, monkey-like face. Kind.

'Now you'll be worried about this big
animal. Your Margie told me you thought she
was tame. Somebody's pet.'

Sammy stiffened. He remembered Sergeant
Hargreaves was only a copper after all. Doing
his duty. Hard luck!

'Sorry,' said Sammy. 'I'm not saying owt!'

The sergeant sighed, and stared out of the window, his helmet still on his knee. He said softly, as if talking to himself. 'She'll not prosper out there. Somebody'll get her in the end. Maybe just wound her, so she'll crawl away and die. Animals suffer terrible, when they crawl away to die. An' what about them cubs of hers? They'd starve to death wi'out her. . .'

Sammy knew it was true. A wave of misery swept over him. He nodded, dumbly.

'Now the place for her,' said Sergeant Hargreaves, 'is in a nice, safe, warm zoo. Where the cubs can grow up in peace. Where you can go an' see her, whenever you want . . .'

Sammy nodded again.

Sergeant Hargreaves seemed to cheer up. 'So if you show us where she's got them . . .'

Sammy gave him a sharp look. He seemed just a bit too eager. 'How will they catch her?' he asked suspiciously.

'Wi' nets, of course. Catch her in a net, put her in a crate, an' off she goes to the zoo.'

'Which zoo?'

'I don't know, yet. Give me a chance.'

Sammy thought his questions worried the sergeant. Quite a lot. So he said. 'When I see the net, an' the crate, an' I've talked to the zoo men, I'll show you where she is.'

'Don't you trust me?' asked the sergeant. He tried to look Sammy in the face with a grin. But it didn't quite work.

'I don't trust nobody any more!' said Sammy.

'I don't blame you, lad. After what you've been through.' The sergeant got up with a heavy sigh, and went downstairs.

*   *   *   *   *

They came the next morning with a big lorry, and a big strong crate in the back. The two men driving wore caps that said 'Dudley Zoo'.

Sammy gave them a hard time, asking all kinds of questions about the zoo, and how they looked after big cats. They seemed to know what they were talking about. But they didn't seem to be taking it seriously. They were a bit shifty. They wouldn't look him in the eye.

But they offered him a lift in their lorry, and there wasn't anything Sammy could do but go

with them. He told them to drive up the green road, to Hoskins'. When they got to Hoskins' farm, Sammy said, 'She's got the cubs in the farmhouse—in the loft,' and he felt a cold horror creep over him as he said it. He felt like Judas Iscariot, betraying Jesus. The cheetah would be waiting for him to bring her breakfast. She'd had nothing yesterday, thanks to stupid Margie. She'd be trusting him, and he was bringing men with nets. She'd be scared. She might panic and fight.

'I'll go in and get her for you,' he added. 'She trusts me. She'll come with me. Then you can go in and get the cubs . . .'

'Leave all that to us, kid,' said the man who'd been driving. His voice had changed, gone rough and bossy. Like once he'd got the news he wanted, Sammy didn't matter any more. 'Just sit still. We'll see to it.'

A sudden suspicion grabbed Sammy. 'Where's your nets?' he asked.

'Never you mind, kid. Just leave it to us.'

'What are you waiting for?'

'Never you mind, kid.' The man laughed, unkindly.

Just then, another lorry, an army lorry, pulled up alongside. A lot of soldiers got out, carrying rifles.

'What are they for?'

'Just in case she tries to escape, kid. Just in case she turns dangerous.'

And now Sammy knew he was lying.

Other cars drew up. A jeep, with an officer in it, and a man with a radio on his back, and a high waving aerial, like a fishing-rod. Then there were farmers' cars and hay trucks and farmers got out, carrying shotguns. Dad was there, though he kept well away from Sammy. He was waving his arms and grinning again, though. Pleased with himself as if nothing had happened.

The soldiers and the farmers made a big circle round the farmhouse. They all pointed their guns at the farmhouse doors and windows.

'Where's your nets,' Sammy asked the zoo men, desperately. 'SHOW ME YOUR NETS!' He was screaming now.

'Ain't no nets, kid,' said the driver. 'She'll have to be shot. She's run wild. She's dangerous.'

'But she's a *pet*. She trusts me. She'll come with me, if I go in the crate with her . . .'

'We can't mess about catching cheetahs, kid. Haven't you heard, there's a war on.'

The officer came across. 'We're going to kick in the door. Throw a few smoke grenades inside. That should fetch her out. If that doesn't work, we'll set fire to the place. OK? You ready? We'll deal with the cubs afterwards.'

Sammy felt like smashing his face in with a big hammer. Smashing in all their stupid faces with a big hammer. But he knew he couldn't do anything. If he made a fuss, they'd just drive him away. And he had to stay with her to the end. Tears began streaming down his face, so he was afraid he wouldn't be able to see.

A soldier walked across and kicked the farmhouse door in. She'd be up there, crouching, listening, afraid. But willing to fight to the death for the cubs.

Then there was a sound of boots, running, thudding on the turf, coming nearer. He looked up. It was the soldier with the radio on his back. He said to the officer, 'New orders sir. Do nothing. Somebody's coming across to check things out. Stand down till he's seen the place.'

'Who the hell?' asked the officer crossly. You could tell he was all set for a bit of fun, killing a cheetah.

'Top brass, sir. *Very* top brass indeed. Direct from HQ Northern Command at York.'

'Damn!' said the officer. 'Everybody stand easy.' The soldiers put down their rifles at their feet, and began to light up cigarettes.

They stood, and they stood, while the sun went across the sky. And still there was no sign of the cheetah. And still Sammy did not let himself hope.

And then they heard one little jeep coming up the green road. There were two men in it. The man who was driving was one-handed. The jeep stopped by Sammy's truck. The man was driving one-handed because he only had one arm. The sleeve of his battledress, where the other arm should be, was pinned up neatly to his shoulder. He only seemed to have one eye, too. At least the other eye had a patch

over it.

And then . . . when the man stepped out of his jeep, it was just as if he stepped out of the newspapers. Only he was in full colour, not black and white. How often had Sammy seen that face in the paper, with the black patch over one eye?

He was a hero; he had won medals, he was called a funny name, a French name, even though he was a British hero. Brig. . .Brigadier Guy Le Fevre VC, DSO. The commando raid on the Lofotens—Abyssinia. The Long Range Desert Group. Lost an eye in the first war, and an arm in the second.

'What's all this nonsense?' said Brigadier Guy Le Fevre. 'Some silly idiot tryin' to shoot my melanoid cheetah?' He strode up to the front door of the farmhouse, and shouted, 'Tenga? Tenga, old girl? Come down this instant and meet the boss!'

There was a long pause. He stood tapping his leg impatiently, with his little stick held in his one good hand.

And then she came, leaping and twisting and fawning with joy and pleasure. And they played in the yard in front of everybody, as if nobody was watching at all.

And then she went back inside and fetched the cubs, carrying them by the neck, one by one, and laying them at his feet.

*   *   *   *   *

After a while, the Brigadier came back to the truck, with all the cheetahs bounding at his heels.

'Who's the laddy who found her then?'

Blushing and silent with awe, Sammy got down stiffly from the truck. He could hardly walk, he was so stiff with the pain in his bottom, and all the awful waiting. He felt a bit sick, too. He was frightened he might be sick over that marvellous smart battledress, with the empty sleeve pinned up, and that purple ribbon of the VC. Tenga saw Sammy, and came across and pushed her wet muzzle into his hand.

'I can see you two are good friends,' said Brigadier Guy Le Fevre. 'And I can see somebody's given you a rare thrashin', too. Wouldn't tell them where she was hiding, eh?'

Sammy nodded. He kept looking at Tenga.
He couldn't bear to look at the great hero.

'But you kept your mouth shut, eh? How'd
you manage that?'

'Thought about something else. Thought
about Tenga.'

'Sound scheme. Usually helps. I've got a lot
to thank you for, young man. Left Tenga with
a friend. Damn bomb got him—Tenga broke
loose. Been lost three months. . . Somebody
showed me an article in the paper—got the

word on the blower this morning. Get her somewhere safe, now. North-west Scotland. No Jerry bombers there.' He fumbled in one of his pockets, pulled out a wallet, and took out a large white note, one-handed, with amazing skill. He offered it to Sammy. Sammy had never seen one like it, but he knew it was money. Five pounds? Ten pounds? Two weeks' wages for Uncle Artie.

He looked up at the great hero for the first time, and shook his head.

'I did it for Tenga. No thanks.'

The piercing eyes looked him up and down. The tight mouth suddenly smiled in under-standing.

'Well, you can go up and see her in Scotland, any time you like. When there's an army lorry goin' up that way. Just give 'em a ring at the barracks at Carlisle . . .'

And then, here was Dad, creeping up with a smile on his face, wanting to be involved, wanting to shake hands with the great hero.

'I'm his Dad, sir.'

The hero stiffened. A bit like Tenga did, when she heard a strange noise. You could somehow tell the hero had killed people, as Tenga had killed sheep and calves.

'You'll be the fool that thrashed him, then?' The hero's voice cut like a knife, a sword, swishing through the air.' Wouldn't do it too often if I was you. He's goin' to be bigger than you are, one day.'

And then he turned his back on Dad. Who stood there sheepishly like a grinning fool, then crept away.

'Must be off, then,' said the hero. 'See you again, sometime, maybe. After the war. If you ever feel like joinin' the army, mention my name.'

He got back into his jeep, and Tenga and the cubs just simply got in the back, in a great huddle, and they all drove away. The soldiers got in their truck and followed him down the green road. Then all the farmers came forward, and shook Sammy by the hand, saying he was famous now.

He didn't say anything. In their other hands they still carried the shotguns that they'd brought to shoot Tenga with. So they grew embarrassed and drove off in a hurry.

He was alone. Far down the green road, he could see Dad walking home alone too. Nobody had offered Dad a lift either. He didn't know what would happen, when he got home. He didn't know what he could ever say to his father again. Sergeant Hargreaves was a liar, and he'd trusted Sergeant Hargreaves. They were *all* liars, wanting to kill Tenga one minute, and then . . .

He hurt. It would be a long painful walk home . . .

But home was the only place you had to go to. So he went.

At least Mam would understand. And Uncle Artie.